Echoes Of Empire

Two Brothers, One Kingdom, Infinite Resolve

Yukt Khetan

Contents

I
The Shattered Kingdom

The curtains swished as soothing moonlight painted my chest silver. I heard the frosty wind outside, making the autumn leaves rustle and scrape across the worn terrain. Waves crashed against the sandy shore while a spine-chilling breeze whispered through the evergreens. A gloomy mist had spread, striking terror in those who dared to watch it. Fate's cruel hand had found its mark. The foggy autumn replaced the usual nocturnal melody with a deafening silence, broken only by the animals accepting their frosty, frigid fate. Darkness wrapped the island as the shadow of impending death loomed ahead.

It was a day of war—a day of death. My father, the King of our clan, had been attacked by the mighty Emperor of West Gradam, Quin-Chi—who killed my uncle and crowned himself. My father had escorted my brother Renid and me to an island for our safety before returning to the mainland to fight. He left us only with a large portrait, an aesthetic scroll, and ten of his loyal warriors.

I tossed and turned, but sleep would not engulf me. I felt something unusual—an indescribable sensation. I looked around. I was alone, or so I thought. Renid was sleeping soundly. I was pulled into my imagination and then snapped back to reality. Darkness, once again. My brain struggled to process what was happening as I slowly rose from my soft goatskin bed. The cold, creaky planks beneath my feet sent a shiver down my spine as I walked across the room. The scroll my father left lay before me atop a wooden bench.

With great effort, I climbed onto the table and reached for a torch. I held the flame close to my face, feeling its heat wash over me—a moment of enlightenment amid the uncertainty.

I eventually got myself to use the torch to light the table lamp. After replacing the torch in its original position, I slid it into its holder. I sat down and picked up my father's picture and admired it. My heart was pounding. My father was a source of great pride—a great king, warrior, and man. I loved him dearly. Mindful that the picture was delicate, I gently placed it down, careful not to damage it. Finally, I picked up the scroll, tugged gently on the ribbon, and slowly unfurled it before I began to read:

Dear Sons,

Emperor Son-He—my father, your grandfather—was a mighty man. He ruled a vast empire divided into two districts of Gradam: the East and the West. He passed these districts on to the throne's heirs—your uncle and me. However, as you know, things took a turn when the notorious Quin-Chi assassinated your uncle and seized control of the West.

In his evil desire to expand his territory, he has been relentlessly attempting to conquer our kingdom, East Gradam. United with our allies, we have stood firm so far. However, he is not the type of op who gives up quickly. He has tried multiple times to persuade our allies to abandon us, promising them freedom. Nothing worked; Our allies were loyal to us. Then, he resorted to bribery.

Eventually, we faced a massive betrayal from our northern allies. They blocked our sea route, rendering our southern allies useless. With that, Quin-Chi began to overpower us with his black jade army and plans to kill me soon. I have sent you to this deserted island to hide your existence, as he also wants to eliminate all heirs to the throne.

Fear not, I am a mighty king and will die a mighty king. We will fight until the last warrior falls. I will die protecting our people, our land, and our kingdom. But you, my sons, must live to avenge our deaths and rebuild the kingdom from its ashes. If you are reading this, it is a significant pride for me. Always remember, even in death, I am with you.

With Love, Your Father

The Emperor of West Gradam

ॐ

My heart skipped a beat, and tears welled up in my eyes. I wanted this to be a cruel lie, a foolish dream, but unfortunately, it was not. Anger coursed through me as I tightened my grip on the scroll. The Thunder roared as fierce as a beast. Meanwhile, lightning crackled across the sky like a raging fire, and rain pounded the shore with immense force. Anger consumed me, and I etched in my heart: *I will avenge you, Father. I will avenge our people, and I will kill him.*

My heart was brimming with sorrow, brutally torn apart. I was broken and felt dead inside. Quin-Chi would have murdered my father by now. That thought made me furious. The mixed emotions of anger, sadness, and despair had complete control over my body.

As the fire in the lamp exhausted itself, the weather eventually calmed, and the rain subsided. I was lost in my thoughts until I finally came to my senses. There was no point in mourning what was over, as nothing could be changed.

I rolled up the scroll and tied the ribbon back around it, ensuring it appeared nothing had happened the previous night. However, my eyes told a different story. Swiftly, I slipped back into bed, and sleep finally engulfed me.

The first rays of sunlight pierced through the window, casting a warm glow across the room; a sense of determination washed over me after the night's stormy events. They had left a noticeable mark, igniting a flame of revenge running deep within my soul. This changed me altogether. As long as I was alive, I had one primary goal: to kill Quin-Chi. With this newfound resolve, I knew my father's death would not go unpunished. I would fulfil his dying wish by avenging his fall, even if it meant battling the mighty King Quin-Chi himself single-handedly. My vision started returning to focus as patches of light entered my eyes. I felt a brief vibration in my ear.

I woke to the crackling of a campfire and the wafting aroma of food. My stomach growled loudly; last night, I had only managed to eat a couple of berries. I closed my eyes again, thinking of taking a quick nap to refresh myself further. But that brief respite turned into an hour. As the aroma grew stronger, I could hear footsteps—many were preparing for the day. Finally, I summoned the energy to sit up, rubbing my eyes to clear the sleep. After a few moments, my vision adjusted to the light. Then came the meal. I was so ravenous that I could have eaten a horse. After laying out all the plates, we began to feast.

Rabbits, pigs, berries, and tomatoes—that was all we had, but it was enough to fill our stomachs. All day, I pondered my father's words. I knew what to do, but I wasn't sure how. Restlessness coursed through me; I needed answers, something to guide me, just as my father had when he taught me to walk. Tears welled up in my eyes. His sacrifice couldn't be in vain, could it?

I knew I couldn't fight Quin-Chi alone. I needed friends I could trust, allies who sought justice and shared my perspective, and who were willing to sacrifice everything to achieve our goals. Fortunately, I had my brother and loyal warriors by my side. Though our resources and troops were limited, we had one thing that could help us defeat Quin-Chi. The one thing that makes a shrivelled heartbeat in the darkness is hope.

A day after the hearty feast, we had only a few berries, rabbits left, and hardly any firewood. Then, a brilliant idea struck me. I decided to explore the forested side of the island. This would allow me to gather firewood and resources, toughen me up, better understand our surroundings, and help us locate a clean water source.

Slowly, I slipped into the forest as I ventured into the deep, dark, dense wood forest. Sunlight filtered through the vast meadows, Towering wooden giants dancing and singing with the wind. They had hundreds of arms stretched out. Every wooden giant was grasping a flower or a fruit. But don't be fooled: the rose may be red and beautiful, yet it is as spiky as a sabre-toothed tiger's fang. The fruit may boast vibrant colours on the outside, but inside, it is as poisonous as a cobra.

Hanging from the trees were vines resembling camouflaged green serpents while a symphony of nightingales chirped in the background, accompanied by the distant crash of a waterfall. A carpet of fallen autumn leaves whispered stories of forgotten eras. The air was filled with the sweet scent of honey and blossoms as leaves drifted down, joining their forefathers on the forest floor. Here, animals lived in peace, and silence reigned.

I took a torch and an axe to explore the vast canopy. Wandering through the forest until dawn, I moved in and out of the shadows. A soft, lapping noise was nearby, and I caught sight of two yellow eyes and a sleek body. I recognised a predator in its gaze—blood, pain, and murder. It was a vicious creature—an apex predator.

It had seen me. It was moving, staring directly at me. If looks could kill, I would already be dead. I could read its thoughts: "Easy prey." It regarded me as if I were dinner or just an evening snack. I swung my axe to scare the creature, holding it defensively in front of me. But it was too fast; I couldn't even get a proper look at it. I thought a rock might do the trick, so I threw one at the creature. It didn't even flinch. Instead, it gently placed its paws on the leaves and twigs without making a sound. It was just me and the beast—nothing and no one in our way—or so I thought.

It was faster than I was and more robust, too. I had nowhere to run, nowhere to hide. I felt helpless, but could I afford to feel that way?

While considering my options, my survival instinct kicked in, urging me to sprint. I ran as if my life depended on it—and it did. This Situation was a do-or-die situation, or perhaps a do-and-die one. I could hear the creature behind me, its gaze fixed as if I were an extra-cheese-loaded, twelve-inch, cheese-stuffed, triple seven-cheese margherita pizza.

As I ran, I spotted a few monkeys in the trees ahead, each clutching a rock. I continued to sprint at first, but then they jumped down and blocked my path.

They tried to assault me, but the creature came in front of me to protect me from the silly monkeys or to claim me as its prey. Either way, it growled at the monkeys, sending them fleeing in fear. To top it all off, I noticed that the monkeys had injured the creature. I gave a low grin to my incredible luck, and now I could flee safely without losing a limb or two.

I raced away but heard a faint noise in the distance—a soft whimper. I tried to escape, leaving the creature to its fate, but something stopped me. As I looked back, I noticed that the beast was in sorrow. I felt I should return and help, even if it meant risking my life. Upon closer inspection, I realised that the creature was a wounded panther. The panther had saved me. Maybe unwillingly, but he did do the deed. He saved me like he was my friend. My father always said,' A friend in need is a friend. I had to help him. I knew that this was a vital favour that I had to repay.

I rushed around, gathering stones and arranging them in a circle. Then, I searched for a hollow stone to use as a pot. I hurried from tree to tree and herb to herb, collecting leaves and berries along the way. I gathered twigs and lit them with my torch to create a campfire, on which I placed my makeshift pot, frequently adding stream water to mix with the herbal remedies in hopes of healing the panther's wounds. I was no expert, but I spent all night trying to heal him. Just as I was about to call it quits at sunrise, the panther finally regained consciousness.

One day, I passed in the forest. As I walked back toward home, the panther followed. He was trying to convey something to me. After a moment, I realised he wanted me to ride him. I climbed onto his back; somehow, he knew exactly where I wanted to go. As we neared the shed-like hut the warriors had built for us, I heard a loud, familiar noise.

It was Renid wailing. As soon as I opened the door, I found Renid both delighted and distraught—happy that I was safe but terrified that the panther would eat us. The guards quickly noticed the commotion and pointed their spears at the panther. After a lengthy explanation, everyone eventually understood how I had befriended the creature.

Then Renid began hooting in different tunes, and a colossal eagle—nearly as giant as Renid's lower body—swooped down to perch on his shoulder. Moments later, two more eagles gracefully followed, landing on his other shoulder and head, each brimming with personality. "What are their names?" I asked, filled with curiosity.

Renid replied, "Pecker, Fetcher, and Chainsaw."

"Wait a second, did you just say Chainsaw?" I asked in astonishment.

"Yes, Chainsaw," he said, a mischievous glint in his eye. "Eventually, you'll see why. What's the name of the panther?"

Spontaneously, I responded, "His name is Shadow. Shadow, the fearsome panther."

I considered taking Renid into battle, but he was the only true heir to the throne beside me. He loved our father profoundly and would want revenge—he would do anything for it. That was, of course, if I told him what was written on the scroll. But his life would be at stake, and I couldn't bear to see that unfold. Too many people had already been lost: my uncle, my grandfather, even my father. I had no choice.

I was never good at keeping secrets, and this one could not be hidden from Renid. He was a brilliant strategist who had even helped our father plot attacks against weak points in the enemy's army. A young prodigy, he had become the best chess player in our kingdom by age five while most children were still learning how to write. He needed to be part of the plan. We should directly attack Quin-Chi and try to trigger a revolt, but my brother might have something else in mind.

There had to be a way to tell him what he didn't know. I approached my brother, who still thought this was just a short vacation soon to end.

"Renid?"

"Yes?" he replied, turning his attention away from feeding Pecker.

"There's something I've been meaning to tell you."

"Well then, go on with it."

"So, there's this thing. You know Father sent us to this island for a brief break while he handled the clan's interests? Well, Quin-Chi attacked our kingdom."

"We have many allies," he replied, casually confident.

Tears began to well in my eyes as I murmured, "He bribed our allies not to interfere." Renid locked his gaze on mine and saw the whole truth.

"No, this can't be happening. It just can't be."

"But it has," I replied, my heart heavy.

Renid spoke firmly, "What has been lost cannot be returned. We cannot change the past. But there is one thing we can change: Quin-Chi's destiny. Time is of the essence. We need to plan. We need to train—train very hard."

It had only been two days since our father left us on the island, though it felt like weeks. Renid woke everyone before sunrise to give a speech. He gathered our father's loyal warriors, their faces etched with sorrow and determination. When everyone was outside the shed-like hut the warriors had constructed for us, Renid began.

"As you all know, the great ruler has taken his last breath. We need to fight back and take revenge. We will not stop until Quin-Chi's heart is pierced. We will fight till the last drop of blood we have."

We worked day and night—training, building, plotting, and strategising. Everyone practised their skills. One of the warriors had been a builder before joining the army; another spoke five languages because he had served as a marine engineer. Eventually, a former cartographer among us sketched a rough map of our location and the nearby areas on the back of the scroll.

It took us about a week and a half to construct a boat. We gathered wild herbs for food and healing. With hearts filled with a burning desire for justice and revenge, we prepared to embark on a perilous journey to the mainland, the land of Gradam.

II
Exile and Resolve

The journey was gruelling. After three days, the worst happened: the weather turned treacherous. Fierce waves threatened to tip over the boat, and lightning struck within inches of us—not once, but twice. Yet, we continued with our unbroken spirits and unwavering determination.

Our tiny boat felt like a rubber duckling adrift on a vast pool, pleading for mercy from the storm's fury. Days, weeks, and even fortnights blurred together; we had lost all sense of time. Holding the crew together was a challenge. Resources dwindled; we scavenged the sea below for food and water—our sole sustenance. The ocean, usually a source of life, ironically became the harbinger of death, unleashing relentless winds while rain wiped away all sense of direction. A groan echoed from the hull—a sickening crack signalling impending doom. Death felt close at hand.

A soldier approached, his face etched with grim certainty.

"Sire," he rasped, "the boat will founder within the hour."

Despair clawed at my throat. This fragile vessel, our last hope, was on the verge of betrayal.

Guilt gripped me. "I dragged Renid into this mess," I whispered, tasting the salt stinging on my lips. "I am weak, Father. I failed you."

Then, just over the horizon, we spotted another ship. The sight sent a ripple of surprise through our crew. Ahead of us loomed a majestic vessel, ten times the size of our own. Carved from the heart of ancient forests, sets of skilled and experienced hands shaped its sun-baked oak. The vessel sliced the turquoise waves like a hot knife through butter. Its towering masts grasped at the wind, straining to unfurl the sails, the colour of a raging storm cloud. Its glinting-like malevolent eyes pierced the water, a silent promise of destruction.

Rows upon rows of oars, manned by battle-hardened warriors in heavy golden armour, armed with spears and iron shields polished like mirrors. Helmeted figures scanned the horizon, eyes as sharp as obsidian blades, ever-ready for any threat. The ship ahead was no mere ship; it was a predator, a floating fortress, a testament to the power and ambition of a lost age. Its hull bore a flag of an unknown kingdom—a silver serpent with gold scales and diamond eyes.

Could this be a friendly vessel, offering safe passage—or were they predators drawn to our vulnerability? My heart pounded. Was this a lifeline or another twist of fate? Renid, perched on Shadow, squinted, studying the approaching ship. Overhead, his eagles—Pecker, Fetcher, and Chainsaw—circled, their sharp eyes scouring the deck for any sign of hostility.

As the ships drifted closer, a tall, blonde man appeared on their deck. The warriors, veterans of countless battles, stood in formation, spears ready. Silence hung heavy in the air, broken only by the howling wind and the groaning of our boat.

"Who dares trespass on the waters of Niap Dnal?" the man's voice boomed, each word echoing across the waves. "Identify yourselves, state your purpose, and prepare to face the consequences!"

"We are Swish and Renid, sons of the Emperor of East Gradam. We seek passage to Gradam to liberate our kingdom from Quin-Chi's rule."

"East Gradam, you say?" The man fell silent for a moment, his gaze unblinking. Then, a slow smile spread across his face as he said, "Guards, seize them."

We were quickly bound in chains. Even Shadow, along with all our belongings, was taken. Darkness swallowed us. Then, a familiar voice broke the silence.

"Swish! Swish, wake up!"

I blinked, my vision blurry. Slowly, my surroundings came into focus. Dim light seeped through cracks in the wooden planks above, revealing a cramped, unfamiliar space. Night had fallen. We were no longer on our battered boat. Wherever we were, it felt like a cage. A cold realisation settled in my stomach. We were trapped.

"I thought you were dead! I thought I'd lost you!" Renid murmured, relief in his voice. "These are soldiers of neighbouring land. They make us work day and night, even Shadow. They feed him rotten fish and scraps. These people are cruel."

My voice came out in a hoarse whisper, "Wait, what?" But a sharp pinch on my arm silenced me.

"Shh!" Renid hissed.

"How long have I been out?"

"About five days," he replied hesitantly.

"Five days!?" I gasped, shocked. Renid lightly slapped my shoulder.

"Be quiet, dummy!" he whispered, his eyes darting nervously toward the guards.

Across the dimly lit chamber, another figure stirred in a nearby cell—a middle-aged man, his face etched with weary defiance. Renid leaned closer, his voice barely a murmur.

"That's the real captain. His corrupt General took control and declared himself King of Niap Dnal."

Renid, the strategist, observed our captors. They were undisciplined. A plan began to take shape in his mind.

Over the next few days, Renid pretended to be weak and compliant. He even offered helpful suggestions to the guards, voluntarily doing extra work and subtly flattering them. He gained their trust, then began using it, manipulating them into revealing their routines and vulnerabilities. He learned about the changing guard schedules and the location of the keys.

One sweltering afternoon, as the guards grew sluggish from the heat, Renid saw an opportunity. He "accidentally" tripped a guard, sending him sprawling. In the ensuing chaos, fueled by newfound determination, I used the wooden planks I'd been forced to carry all day to pry open the flimsy lock on our cage.

The real captain, a man named Theon, watched in disbelief. Renid, with a quick wink, asked me to explain our Situation and his plan to Theon. Theon looked amazed, his eyes glittering like never before.

"Young boy, you are brilliant. I wish we had more people like you in my kingdom!" he exclaimed proudly.

In the flickering light, Theon saw me, Renid, as two young brothers and loyal warriors filled with courage and cunning. Surprised and disoriented, I quickly subdued the guards while perched on Shadow's back. Theon guided us through the ship with calculated steps and smooth manoeuvres, keeping our advance organised and precise.

Theon captured the General, who had once held him captive. The General cowered, a whimper slipping from his cracked lips.

"Your time is up, wretch," Theon rasped, his voice a gravelly whisper choked with years of stifled fury.

"Please..." the General choked out. "Spare me."

Theon's usual gentle eyes had transformed. Once soothing blue, his irises now blazed like red-hot embers, the whites darkened and veined with fury. "Spare you? Like you spared the innocent lives, you crushed under your iron fist? Like you spared my men?" His voice cracked on the last word, a tremor running through his weathered frame.

"I... I have a family," the General whimpered a pathetic plea that died in the still air.

Theon scoffed—a humourless sound that scraped against Renid's nerves. "And so did I. Before you ripped them from this world for your own blasted gain." A glint of steel flashed in the dim light as Theon drew his spear. The soldier's whimper turned into a high-pitched scream that echoed through the ship, bouncing off the damp stone walls. But Theon remained unmoved.

Theon held the spear aloft for a long, agonising moment, the weight of the dead and the promise of safety etched into his face. Then, with a final groan, he released the soldier, who collapsed to the floor in a heap, blood staining his mouth and his pierced, greedy heart.

The silence in the chamber was deafening, broken only by Renid's horrified breaths. The brutal act hung heavy in the air, a grim reminder of the cost of our rebellion. But it was also a symbol of resolve. There would be no mercy for those who had brought such suffering. We would fight fire with fire, and blood would stain the path to our liberation.

Humbled by our bravery, Theon revealed a shocking truth: his land, Niap Dnal, bordered Gradam. He, too, had suffered from Quin-Chi's treachery. The "black jade army" that had plagued my father was funded, in part, by resources stolen from Theon's kingdom.

When we finally reached the shores of Niap Dnal, a collective cheer erupted from our weary crew as the land stretched out before us. News of Theon's return and our daring escape had preceded us, and the people greeted us with relief and admiration. But this wasn't the only surprise we witnessed.

We met a rugged, weary-looking boy who seemed a couple of years older at the palace doors than me. He walked with a sense of prideful determination. After he met King Theon, we learned that he was the prince of Niap Dnal—the King's son who had gone into hiding after the General had taken over. His name was Hercule.

After our introduction to Hercule, we prepared ourselves as the town laid out a feast fit for heroes—heroes we had indeed become. The meal was no ordinary celebratory but a symphony of flavours, a legendary Niap Dnal spread.

Each dish was a masterpiece, a delicacy in its own right—slow-roasted rabbit, goat, pig, and chicken drizzled with fragrant herbs and spices worldwide. Pastries filled with sweet, spiced jams and jewel-like fruits unlike any I had ever seen. Soups that melted like gold on the tongue.

To quench our thirst, chefs passed around chilled glasses of iced mango lassi; the sweet, tangy nectar was the perfect counterpoint to the rich flavours of the food. The first bite was a dream; it felt like the last should never come. Each taste was an explosion that danced on my tongue, every bite worth its weight in gold. It was as if every legend I'd heard about Niap Dnal's cuisine had been confirmed—an experience so divine it could have brought tears to my eyes if exhaustion hadn't already claimed them all.

The banquet hall was magnificent, stretching as long as the gateway of China—golden cups, intricately carved and embedded with gems, glimmered under the captivating and colourful lights.

The silver plates were polished to mirrors, and the bronze was a sparkling star. Renid raised his glass mid-fast and spoke loudly, "A toast". The hall chanted the same thing within minutes, voices rising in unison.

The King rose, commanding the hall's attention. "Silence, my friends!" His voice echoed through the hallway; even though he was aged, he held an undeniable command. He raised his golden goblet high, the light catching on its intricate carvings, casting elaborate shadows across the hall. "Tonight, we have gathered not just to celebrate my return but also to honour heroes!" He paused, letting the weight of his words sink in, his confident tone full of meaning.

"The heroes who dared to defy evil, who stared death in the face and emerged victorious. But heroism, my friends, comes in many forms. It is not always in the clash of steel or the roar of battle. Sometimes, it lies in the quiet strength of a strategist, the mind that anticipates danger and carves a path even in the darkest hours." He took a small sip before continuing, his gaze locking with mine across the hall.

"Tonight, we raise our goblets to honour Prince Swish! His cunning mind helped unravel the grip of the corrupt. His foresight allowed me, Prince Renid, and the other warriors to break free and ignite the spark of rebellion!"

A cheer erupted, louder than before, filled with genuine admiration. Knights pounded their goblets on the table, the rhythmic clang echoing through the hall. With a smile on his weathered face, Theon raised his goblet again. "To Swish, the strategist! May his mind ever be sharp, his loyalty unwavering, and his name forever engraved in the history of Niap Dnal. On this occasion, I will knight him. Bring forth the mythical knighting sword!"

There were collective gasps among the crowd; never had such a young boy of ten been knighted. A small troop entered a nearby room, returning with a sword on a golden platter with a red cushion.

The King spoke with pride. "Come forward, Swish."

As I prepared to step forward, I heard a minister grumble under his breath, muttering to another nearby, "I served him before he was even King. Twenty-one years I've worked for him, and this fool he's only known for a week is to be knighted? What's next—will my one-month-old child be crowned King?"

Though I was meant to approach, I stood rooted to the spot and spoke loudly, "I cannot accept this knighting."

Another murmur rose, accompanied by hushed comments from the crowd. "Unbelievable. The boy is offered a once-in-a-lifetime honour, and he denies it," whispered one minister, incredulous.

The crowd gasped again, and the King was momentarily speechless, taken aback. "Why, son? You deserve this honour. You may not know it, but many would sacrifice for such recognition. Come now; it is rightfully yours."

I looked up at him and replied, "No, honourable King. With due respect, I cannot accept it. While I revealed the plan to you, my brother, Prince Renid, conceived it. I believe he is the one most deserving of this honour."

The crowd let out a third collective gasp. The King turned to my brother. "Is this true, Prince Renid?"

My brother replied tearfully, "Yes, Your Majesty."

The King was astonished. "Such honesty is rare; you two princes alone are worth more than the entire treasury of the kingdom."

Nearby, the minister murmured jealously, "He's known them for a week, and now they're valued more than the entire treasury. Niap Dnal is one of the wealthiest kingdoms—not some small province."

The King rested his sword on Renid's shoulder and declared, "King Theon of Niap Dnal at this moment knights Prince Renid of East Gradam and shall be known henceforth as Sir Renid of East Gradam." A tear rose in my eyes as the crowd broke into applause. I knew that if Father were here, he'd be proud. But he wasn't, and I still had to avenge him.

After the applause subsided, everyone returned to rest for the night. We convened a meeting the following day to plan our strategy against Quin-Chi. Four of us gathered: Renid, Theon, me, and Hercule.

Renid said, "We have a temporary haven here, but it won't last long. Quin-Chi craves power—he needs both wealth and land. Guess who holds the most of each and is nearest to his territory?"

I answered quietly, "Niap Dnal. That means we'll be his next target."

"No," said Hercule. "Look at the pattern. Quin-Chi only attacks lands with armies far weaker than his, almost tenfold smaller. He thrives on fear, using it to grow stronger."

"We must kill him before he grows stronger," I said quickly, trying to steer away from the looming negativity.

"Patience, brother," Renid replied thoughtfully. "We have about seventeen days before he turns on us: three days to conquer the northeastern islands, six for the northern territories, where he will surely betray their trust, and six more to return to a nearby front. One day for rest and another for regrouping and preparation."

I spoke in horror, "Seventeen days... that's all?"

"No," Hercule corrected. "Our army can hold him off for an additional three days. After that, we'll be out of options, three days closer to the inevitable."

"No," Renid said confidently. "We can hold him off for a little longer with interference."

"Interference?" I asked, intrigued.

"Yes, interference is one of our two key strategies," he replied.

"First, we will have the warriors from the northeastern islands surrender to Quin-Chi when he attacks. Once he conquers their land, they will serve as our spies within his corrupt regime. They'll carry out covert operations, working to sabotage Quin-Chi at every opportunity. Their mission will be to expose his true nature, showing that he rules with an iron fist, not a guiding hand. Will sow doubt among his warriors, weakening their resolve and buying us precious time."

"Second, when he begins plotting against us, we'll offer him a peace offering: the legendary Niap Dnal feast. This gesture will disrupt his plans, making us seem weaker and buying us even more time."

I was left speechless; my brother's sharp mind had grown brilliant. Father would be proud if he were here. But a lingering doubt arose. "A peace offering?" I questioned. "That would surely be suspicious."

King Theon nodded in agreement as Hercule mumbled, "The Niap Dnal feast you just had is expensive. Though we can afford it, wouldn't our resources be better allocated to military expenditures? The offer would likely be declined and might raise doubts. Our soldiers might also question the wisdom of such a decision."

Renid determinedly replied, "While that may be true, you're overlooking the most critical element besides money, men, and resources."

"What's the most important thing?" I asked, barely containing my suspense.

Renid replied in a dark, brooding tone, "Time. The more time we have, the more resources we can gather, the more soldiers we can train, and the more allies we can forge."

Theon tugged at his moustache and said, "So if we gain about 15 days... But how does that truly help?"

"I don't know precisely," Renid replied, "but it gives us just over a month to train, strategise, and prepare. King Theon, I hope you'll ensure our message reaches the northeastern islands. Meanwhile, we'll train the soldiers and approach the Western allies who turned traitor to convince them to join us."

"Why would they ever agree to that?" I asked.

After cracking his knuckles, Renid replied, "They will."

I nodded. "Very well. I trust your judgment. We'll leave tomorrow at dawn to meet the western King of Wadan. It will take us five days to reach him, and we don't have a minute to waste. King Theon, we request your help with the necessary preparations and supplies."

The King asked, "How many men do you need?"

"None. Just my brother and me," I answered quietly.

"Should I send a larger chariot for more food and comfort?" the King offered generously.

Before I could answer, Hercule interjected, "No offence, but it would be wiser to travel on foot. A chariot would draw attention and slow you down across rough terrain."

Renid added, "Besides, a chariot would only soften us, and there's no room for softness in war. That expense would be better used for training or acquiring superior equipment."

"Well said," the King agreed.

Renid and I prepared to embark on an extraordinary journey.

III
Three Trials of Terror

We crossed snow-capped mountains, their peaks touching the clouds and valleys that plunged deep into the earth. We faced raging rivers, gentle streams, vast plains, and lush meadows, enduring everything from bone-chilling cold to the blistering heat of the desert. In the end, we overcame every obstacle.

We were denied entry when we reached the palace of Wadan in the western lands.

"What now?" I asked.

Renid pointed subtly. "Look, a pigeon."

The guard scoffed, laughing mockingly. "Oh, young boy, I've seen that trick before."

I realised Renid was creating a distraction. Seizing the opportunity, I struck the guard, knocking him unconscious. We slipped inside before anyone noticed.

We entered the King's meeting room through the most significant door. I began, "Your Majesty, we need your help—"

But before I could say more, the guards seized us, covering our mouths.

The King regarded us with mild disdain. "Give these poor boys some money and send them away." I struggled, but they held us firmly.

"Release them," the King commanded after a pause. The soldiers obeyed but kept their spears pointed at our heads.

"What do you want, young boys?" the King asked.

Renid replied boldly, "We seek your alliance in the battle against Quin-Chi."

The King chuckled. "Did Quin-Chi send you here to test my loyalty? He is the crafty one."

"No," Renid said, his voice firm. "Quin-Chi isn't your ally. He's using you to gain power. You mean nothing to him; he cares only for your wealth and how you can serve his plans. He allied with the North and then betrayed them. He'll do the same to you. Join us, or face destruction."

The King's expression darkened as he considered this. "Hmm... You boys seem to know much. Are you certain he would betray me?"

"Yes," I answered with urgency. "Quin-Chi has betrayed every ally before you."

The King nodded slowly. "Very well, I'll ally with you—on one condition. You must pass three of my trials. Succeed, and my entire army will be at your command. Fail, and it will cost you your life. We begin in five minutes. Beware—failure means death."

Five minutes felt like an eternity as we were ushered into a separate chamber, the air thick with tension. Renid, usually full of energy, stood uncharacteristically still.

"Three trials," I whispered. "What do you think they'll be?"

He shrugged, a flicker of doubt crossing his face for the first time. "Strength? Strategy? Maybe riddles or puzzles..."

The heavy oak door creaked open, and Captain Zahir entered; his immense size, matched by his steely expression, he announced, devoid of warmth, "The first trail is - The Gauntlet. It will be held in the Chamber of Strength."

He gestured toward a doorway at the far end of the room. We exchanged a glance, both curious and apprehensive, then stepped through. The Gauntlet was a long, narrow corridor lined with masked figures, each holding a different weapon: a spiked mace, a curved scythe, a barbed axe.

"Your task is to pass through this corridor successfully," Zahir instructed.

A booming gong sounded, signalling the start of the trial. The first figure lunged with a spear. Renid ducked swiftly, pulling me low, and we scrambled to our feet as the corridor turned into a chaotic test of offence and defence.

Renid's speed surprised me as he darted through the hall, deftly manoeuvring around opponents. I relied on brute strength, deflecting heavier blows with shields scattered along the corridor.

When I thought we couldn't withstand another attack, the corridor opened into a small chamber at the end. We stumbled inside and collapsed onto the cool stone floor, gasping for breath.

Captain Zahir appeared in the doorway, his stern gaze softened by a hint of respect. "Congratulations," he said. "You've survived the first trial of strength. Prepare yourselves—the second awaits."

A wave of relief washed over me, momentarily erasing the pain in my aching muscles. We had cleared the first hurdle, but two more remained. What new challenges awaited us, and more importantly, would we have the strength and wit to overcome them all?

We barely had a moment to catch our breath before Captain Zahir returned, taking us into a brightly lit chamber. Unlike the Gauntlet's cold stones and dim torches, this room was a scholar's sanctuary, lined floor-to-ceiling with towering bookshelves packed with leather-bound tomes. An ornately carved wooden table stood at the centre, and a single chessboard awaited it.

"Welcome," an old man said in a husky and kind voice. "This is the Chamber of Strategy. Here, your minds—not your bodies—will be tested."

He gestured toward the board. "This is a game of Chess, an ancient test of logic and foresight. One of you will play this trial. If successful, the other of you will need to face the final trial."

A flicker of surprise crossed Renid's face, though he quickly composed himself. "But wouldn't it be more effective to combine our skills?" he asked.

The older man chuckled, a raspy sound. "Perhaps. But sometimes, the greatest strength lies in knowing your weaknesses. This is your challenge."

Renid, always quick on his feet, looked slightly out of place in this scholarly setting. I, however, felt an unexpected pull toward the chessboard.

A silent understanding passed between us. The first trial had tested strength, and this trial would test wit. We reasoned that the third trial would likely test something else entirely—something Renid, with his versatility, was best suited for.

I took the seat across from the best player of the Western Kingdom, feeling the weight of the chess pieces in my hands. The game began—a silent, intense battle of strategy and deduction unfolding on the checkered board. Hours melted away as both the players focused on outsmarting the other, anticipating moves and exploiting weaknesses.

The room was thick with tension, broken only by the occasional clink of a piece as it moved. We were so engrossed in the game and the silent communication that we barely noticed Captain Zahir returning with a faint smile of amusement on his face.

Finally, after what felt like an eternity, I sighed, having cornered my opponent's King with no escape. "Checkmate," I said slowly as tension deflated like a punctured balloon.

The older man nodded, a glimmer of satisfaction in his eyes. "Well played, you've demonstrated impressive skills. He turned to Renid. "Together, you and your brother have conquered the Chamber of Strength and the Chamber of Strategy. Prepare yourself. The final trial awaits."

I was led to a nearby room to wait. Three hours later, Renid burst in, huffing and puffing. Taking a moment to catch his breath, he finally spoke. "The last trial was in the Chamber of Speed. I had to run an obstacle course. They gave me 150 minutes to cross it. Breathtaking task, if you ask me."

Captain Zahir came in briefly. His tone was neutral but tinged with approval. "You have successfully finished all three trials: Strength Strategy and Speed. You have demonstrated a series of talents and endured lots of suffering, both physical and mental. Your efforts have paid off, and you will receive an hour of rest before the King meets you."

After Captain Zahir left, Renid softly mumbled, "Get me some water." I rolled my eyes but hurried off to fetch him some. As I filled a cup with cool water, the soothing sound of it pouring into it filled the silence. Turning off the tap, I prepared to head back, but a sudden loud crash echoed through the room.

Before I could react, a sharp pain shot through my leg. Renid rushed over but slipped on the spilt water from the cup and toppled onto me, sending us both crashing to the floor.

Pain radiated through my leg as my vision blurred. Renid groaned as he landed hard on top of me, leaving us dazed and sprawled out.

"Renid!" I moaned, wincing as I tried to move. My leg throbbed intensely, but after a moment of panic, I realised it wasn't broken—just bruised and sore. Relief washed over me like an incredible wave.

Renid sat up slowly, his expression full of concern. "Are you okay? I landed pretty hard on you."

"My leg hurts like crazy," I replied, inspecting the damage. "Just a bruise, I think. But there's a pretty bad cut running down to my ankle."

He helped me sit up, wincing from his sore leg. "Looks like we both took a hit," he said, attempting a joke that fell flat. I couldn't help but crack a smile despite the pain. We were a mess, but we were alive. And together.

"What was that loud crash?" I asked, glancing at the broken cup on the floor.

Renid grinned sheepishly. "Knocked over a vase rushing for water. Hopefully, it wasn't valuable."

I swallowed the pain and tried to sound braver than I felt. "We need to get ready."

Renid's expression turned serious. "We've come too far to stop now. But first, we must find something to wrap these injuries—before the guards show up."

"And also...?" I prompted, noting the sudden urgency in his voice.

"Look behind you," he said, his tone sharp.

I turned and froze. Floating on the spilt water was a polished silver knife, its gleaming edge sharp and deadly. It must have been hidden inside the vase. Attached to it was a damp piece of paper. Carefully, I picked it up and read the smudged writing:

"In three days, we shall assassinate the King. No one will suspect us. I have worked as his cleaner for years, and he trusts me completely. If you agree, sign below."

The rest of the note was smudged in red ink. Of course, the note had to fall into the water so it would become impossible to decipher.

Renid and I exchanged a look, our bruises and pain forgotten. Someone had intended to use this weapon against the King. We had to act quickly.

We rushed to report the discovery to the King. After reading the note, he leaned back on his throne, his face thoughtful. "Interesting," he murmured. Then, turning to his guards, he commanded, "Guards, summon the royal cleaner now."

The cleaner was brought to the throne room, looking nervous and pale.

The King addressed him, his voice resonant in the hall. "Ah, my trusted cleaner, you've served me loyally over the years."

"Yes, Your Majesty," the cleaner stammered.

The King's tone darkened. "Good, because if I were to discover that you planned to assassinate me with an accomplice, I would be most displeased. So displeased that I might order both of you executed."

The cleaner broke into a cold sweat, his knees buckling. "It was a mistake! Please, Your Majesty, spare me! I'll forgo my wages for the next ten years!"

The King's eyes narrowed, cold fury replacing his initial calm. "You think sparing your wages would please me? I have more than enough wealth. Your betrayal, not the loss of money, broke my trust." He turned to his guards. "Take him away and have him executed for this treachery."

"Please spare me! I'm sorry!" screamed the royal cleaner as the guards dragged him out. His cries echoed in the throne room, but the King remained unmoved.

The King turned to us, a look of gratitude in his eyes. He seemed relieved and also jubilant. "Young men, you saved my life. I am forever in your debt. Tell me—how can I repay you?"

I stood tall, ignoring the ache in my leg. "All we ask, Your Majesty, is that you join us in our battle against Quin-Chi. Together, we will defeat him."

"And so it shall be," replied the King with determination.

He turned to his guards. "Begin an immediate investigation. Leave no one unchecked. I want every person in the kingdom questioned, from the youngest to the oldest. No one is to go without scrutiny. Triple the security and have the guards work double shifts for the next two days—pay them extra for their efforts."

"Yes, sir," the guards replied in unison.

"From this moment on, we are united against Quin-Chi. We will fight the last man if we must," said the King.

IV
Forging the Alliance

Upon reaching Niap Dnal, The people met us with a hero's welcome. Tales of our success- daring escapes and cunning strategies -had spread like wildfire among young and older people, igniting a new hope. Theon, whose face had been lined with worry, was now relieved as he rushed to our side.

After the long journey across unforgiving terrain and harrowing trials, we gathered for a strategy meeting before delivering our peace offering.

"How do we even approach their camp?" I asked Renid and Hercule. "They'll never let us walk in so easily."

"One way is to offer them money," Hercule suggested.

Renid shook his head. "Quin-Chi is already too rich for that to work."

Meanwhile, news of the assassination attempt on the Western King of Wadan had reached Niap Dnal, sending ripples of fear through the kingdom. Theon, ever the strategist, saw a chance to motivate his troops and rally his allies.

"Quin-Chi's treachery has no limits," Theon proclaimed to the assembled council and people. "He spreads distrust, tearing apart not only alliances but also the hearts of the people of his kingdom. This attempt on the Western King's life is proof of his desperation. He fears our unity—and we shall use that against him."

Theon gestured toward Renid and me. "These young heroes, after enduring unimaginable trials, uncovered the assassination plot on the Western King. Their courage and loyalty are a testament to what Niap Dnal stands for."

The council erupted in agreement, and I felt pride balanced by the weight of the mission ahead.

We formed an alliance—**The Protectors**—uniting Niap Dnal, the Western Wadan, the Southwestern Aliened, and the Northeastern islands. A banner of light blue with two clasped hands became our symbol. Word of Quin-Chi's betrayal and the attempt to subvert the Wadan's strength reached the Northeastern islands, sparking rebellion among soldiers and civilians. It indicated that Quin-Chi feared our combined power. He believed we might have a chance to overthrow his Black Jade Army. Once again, our hearts were brimming with optimism.

So far, multiple protests and riots in the northeastern islands have delayed Quin-Chi's plans to attack Niap Dnal for at least a few days.

I spoke grimly, "The Northern Niap Dnal, the Western Wadan, the Southwestern Aliened, and the Northeastern Islands—all united, yet still short of the needed forces. That's a sign of trouble."

"We must act swiftly," Theon added. "But we cannot simply march into their camp. We can't win by sheer numbers alone; we need strategy and reform."

The King of Wadan said, "Fortunately, I have a plan. Has anyone here heard of the D.O.D.?"

I frowned in confusion. "No, I haven't. Why would I know about the D.O.D.?"

All the people in the room looked taken aback, some ministers coughing in surprise. An elder among them cleared his throat and explained, "The D.O.D., or Dealers of Death, was a covert organisation of handpicked soldiers—elite warriors trained as spies and assassins who were sent to opponents' kingdoms. Each one was powerful enough to take down an entire squadron single-handedly. Even a small squad of ten D.O.D. operatives could decimate a small army. The organisation once boasted a force of 100 spies and 850 agents, yet it had no known headquarters. You never know—of the people in this room, there may be Someone who was either an agent or spy of theirs. The D.O.D. fell when Quin-Chi assassinated their leader."

Another minister replied urgently, "The D.O.D. is a thing of the past. The once well-known organisation has no members left."

The King of Wadan smirked and spoke, "Are you sure? Enter my friend."

Suddenly, the doors opened. A dense wall of smoke entered as a figure emerged from the smoke, clad in a suit as dark as midnight with segmented leather straps for agility and ease of movement. A brown belt wrapped around his waist held an array of strange vials and glass bottles. A hood of deep blue obscured most of his face, leaving only a single, piercing red eye visible—a gaze that seemed to hold secrets no mortal should ever know. A red shawl covered his mouth, muffling his voice and concealing his identity further.

"The Rising Raven (TRR) spares no one. No one has insulted me and lived to tell the tale." With that, he raised his dagger—a weapon known as the Ravenblade, infamous for its deadly history. The handle bore a raven carved at one end; its leather grip was wrapped with a strip of red cloth. The blade's edge was rusted, tainted by countless battles, and emitted a metallic, putrid scent, like decaying iron and rot.

TRR started, "I don't work for free. But this one time, I shall make an exception. My grudge against Quin-Chi runs deep—he killed my brother, the leader of the D.O.D. I was never the target; it was my twin who sacrificed himself to save me. And now, I will eliminate anyone who stands in my way to Quin-Chi."

"Very well. Shall we launch the Attack on Quin-Chi, then?" Theon asked.

"No, not yet," Renid replied. "We will proceed in three phases. Phase one: we send a diplomat to propose a peaceful solution and friendship. Quin-Chi will reject it, of course. It's merely a distraction. We distribute rations to his soldiers—some laced with poison. Phase two: some of us will journey to the southern kingdoms to seek the aid of more allies. The Southern navy will be a crucial counterpoint to the strong Black Jade Cavalry. Phase three: ..." He paused, a slight smirk on his face. "Let's keep that part a mystery, shall we?"

"What could you possibly need to hide from us?" Hercule asked, intrigued.

I interjected, "Perhaps it's better if Renid keeps that to himself. If the parts of the plan are revealed in the right order, they can lead to more productive outcomes. We must cooperate. This scenario is our only way out of doom."

"Without further delay, let's embark on this journey," said Hercule. "Let the Gradam brothers go to Quin-Chi's land. Meanwhile, TRR and I will head south to rally more allies."

"No," TRR interrupted. "I already have agents embedded everywhere—even in Quin-Chi's court. I must go myself to handle things directly."

I asked, "How will you breach the impenetrable fortress of Quin-Chi?"

TRR gave a knowing smile. "Trust me, I have my ways. There's an unguarded window on the western wing, sector five."

Hercule looked stunned while the Western King of Wadan nodded deeply.

"Let me prepare," the King of Wadan said. "I should be the diplomat. Quin-Chi knows me well and trusts me. I can stall him for as long as you need. You, meanwhile, do whatever is necessary."

"Then it's settled," Theon said as he cracked his knuckles. "I will accompany my son to the south to secure their alliance while you fulfil your errands. We should ideally meet in about 15 days. Meanwhile, the King of Southwestern Aliened will train our troops."

V
Shadows of Betrayal

Dear Quin-Chi,

The legendary TRR has escaped your attacks and remainsalive. He has an agent embedded in your court. Don't lethim escape, or he'll reveal our alliance, and your plans forworld conquest will stay just that—a dream. The WesternKing of Wadan is still alive, thanks to the meddling. Theyplot to delay you. Let them stall. I know when they'llstrike, but wait for my command before you move. I'mheading south to deal with my father. TRR plans to breachyour castle through an unguarded window in Sector 5 ofthe west wing.

Stay vigilant, Quin-Chi. Do not fail me. One mistake,and I will replace you. Don't get cocky. Remember, I amyour master. So, no funny business.

Fondest Regards,
Hercule

Hercule rolled up the letter and attached it to a carrier bird. Just then, a cleaner who overheard him gasped and muttered, "Master Hercule... How could you betray us like this?"

"Oh, no, you don't," Hercule replied with a cold smile, shoving the cleaner off the balcony. "Oops, guess I accidentally killed him."

A few hours later, Theon set out on his diplomatic mission, and the food was prepared.

Renid devised a secret plan for us to infiltrate Quin-Chi's fortress by hiding in a food crate. Once inside the fortress, we will reveal our existence, which would spark a revolt against Quin-Chi, as he claimed no natural heir to the throne. This revolt would be followed by freeing the prisoners of war and asking them to help us defeat Quin-chi and overthrow him.

We settled into the crates, and hours passed while we made our way toward the gates of Quin-Chi's wicked, self-proclaimed empire. He had arrogantly taken the title: *The King of All Kings, Quin-Chi I.*

We could organise safe passage up to the kingdom's border, but ahead, we spotted guards. We held our breath, forcing ourselves to remain so silent that even breathing was inaudible. We even steadied our heartbeats, softening them to a slow, quiet rhythm.

The guards began inspecting each crate.

A guard opened the crate ahead of us. This was followed by a guard's flat, disinterested voice calling, "Next."

"What do we do?" I whispered, my nerves taut. For the first time in days, I saw a flicker of doubt cross Renid's face. He looked thoughtful, then asked, "Do you trust me?"

I managed a shaky grin. "Well, I'm crammed in a crate of tomatoes with my brother, trying to infiltrate the madman's empire. You think Someone who didn't trust you would ever do that?"

Renid smirked. "Then wait for it."

A creak echoed through the air, and I caught a sliver of glinting moonlight—a comforting sight that always filled me with a sense of calm. Just then, the guard caught sight of us, and his eyes widened. The guard was alarmed to see us. He opened his mouth to shout, but a mysterious figure dragged him back before he could make a sound.

I saw a figure step forward, wearing the uniform and mask of the same guard just knocked down. He removed the mask and winked before cowering it again. Then, mimicking the guard's voice flawlessly, he announced, "All clear. Next!"

It took me a moment to realise—it was TRR.

With his help, we finally made it inside the kingdom walls. I peeked through a hole in the crate, scanning for more guards. "The north and east are clear," I whispered.

Renid responded, "West is clear too, but the South has one guard."

"We can take him," I replied confidently.

Moments later, Another guard pushed us to crate into a storage room. We slipped out quietly, and I moved quickly to silence the guard. But I was a little late—he uttered a piercing scream and raised the alarm within seconds. Armed men swarmed toward us, shackles clinking in their hands. One lunged at me, gripping me tightly, but Renid knocked him out with a swift blow. Before collapsing, though, he managed a brutal kick to my legs.

"Ahhhh!" I yelled, pain shooting through me.

"Let's get out of here before more guards arrive!" Renid urged, eyeing the incoming reinforcements.

"I... I agree," I replied, wincing.

But while Renid sprinted off without hesitation, I could not move. My leg wouldn't budge; Someone was holding it tight.

I tried to turn, but darkness crept in at the edges of my vision, my strength draining away. Within moments, everything faded to black.

Once again, I was swallowed by oblivion.

VI
The Divine Weapon

Meanwhile, Theon and his son Hercule journeyed to the south, where a grand feast was held in honour of their arrival.

Theon asked the Southern King, "What must we do to earn your alliance?"

"We have rivals on our borders who, long ago, stole our legendary bow and arrow—the 'God Set.' These weapons hold great religious significance for us. It's said that the moon god gifted us the 'Moonbow,' and the sun god gave us the 'Arrow of Flames.'"

"But isn't this 'godly bow and arrow' just a myth?" Hercule asked, intrigued.

"No, young man," replied the Southern King. "The God Set is as real as you and me. Retrieve it, and our kingdom will be forever in your debt."

"Then I shall do it. But where can we find this 'God Set'?" Theon asked.

"It is unguarded in the king's chamber," answered the Southern King.

"Unguarded?" Hercule exclaimed, incredulous. "Then why haven't you retrieved it yourselves?"

"Yes, one of the world's most powerful weapons lies unguarded, but we refuse to touch it," the Southern King explained solemnly. "We are deeply religious, and the God Set is encased in thin glass adorned with sun and moon images. Breaking it would mean violating our beliefs."

"Very well. I'll go," Theon said resolutely. "But how many men will join us on this mission?"

"None," the Southern King responded, his voice a mix of resolve and regret. "It lies in a neighbouring land, close by."

"Understood. I'll leave in an hour—provide me with a map. I have my armour ready."

Soon after, Theon prepared for his journey, donning a clever disguise. Within an hour, even Hercule wouldn't have recognised him. He wore oversized, worn-out, torn, and patched clothes, and his once-clean face was now smeared with mud. His hair was ruffled and wild, and his feet were covered in broken, dirty slippers. He held a small dish with a few weathered coins and wrapped an old green scarf around his neck, adding to his dishevelled appearance.

In this guise, Theon looked like a perfect beggar, unassuming and easily overlooked. No one would suspect he was trying to retrieve the legendary God Set.

"Here's the map. Am I right in assuming you intend to go alone, without your son?" the King asked, handing Theon a scroll.

"Yes, I'll go alone. This could easily be a death mission, and one wrong move could prove fatal. My son needs more experience. Besides, if we both went and somehow didn't return, Niap Dnal would be left without a ruler," Theon replied firmly.

"A wise ruler always thinks of his people," the King approved.

"And he'll be safe here... right?" Theon muttered a hint of sarcasm in his voice.

The King chuckled. "No, he won't."

Theon set out for the nearby bordered kingdom and soon reached the gates.

"Halt! You may go no further; turn back to where you came from," commanded a guard with a weary voice.

"I just came here for the free food," Theon said, adopting his best beggar's tone.

The guard rolled her eyes. "I'm so tired of wealthy folks pretending to be poor for a free meal," she said, displaying her calloused, burn-scarred hands.

"But that's none of my concern. Go on through."

Theon's eyes narrowed as he asked, "Your hand—what happened?"

The guard quickly concealed her hand beneath her robe, a single tear slipping from her eye before she brushed it away with a calm, resolved nod.

"Weird..." Theon murmured under his breath as he continued inside the kingdom.

As he walked, leaves rustled beneath his feet. Ahead of him rose a towering castle fortified with iron walls and thick oak beams. The wooden base was intricately carved with scenes of ancient tales, and metal statues of valorous warriors stood guard around the iron fortress. Nearby stone fortresses were shrouded in vines and trees, nature blending seamlessly with architecture. It was a stunning harmony of craft and wilderness—a dreamscape for any architect.

As Theon walked ahead into the kingdom, he saw saddening things everywhere: children were chained, and their parents were forced to work tirelessly for the children's safety. Theon thought this kingdom might boast wonders, but honestly, a king is not defined by his wealth or castle. He is represented by his values, morals and, most of all, his care for his people.

Ahead, a long line of impoverished citizens waited, and guards handed out stale food at the front. Perched above them, encased in glass and resting on a red cushion adorned with sun and moon symbols, were the legendary 'Moonbow' and 'Arrow of Flames.'

After nearly an hour in line, Theon finally reached the front. In one swift motion, he punched through the glass and seized both the Moonbow and Arrow of Flames. Within moments, armed guards surrounded him, their spears pointed at his neck.

"Surrender now, or these spears will taste blood," commanded a general.

But Theon was two steps ahead. "I'd think twice before attacking," he countered. "Unless you want to see this wooden castle ablaze in moments. I'll use the God Set if you don't surrender."

The General's eyes widened in shock, realising he had been outmanoeuvred. "Weapons down!" he barked reluctantly, and the soldiers dropped their spears. He then asked, "What is it you seek? Money? Power? Land?"

"Only the God Set," Theon replied with confidence. But then, a thought struck him. "And one more thing... stop torturing these innocent people. Because if you don't, you may wake up in hell sooner than you think."

The general, rattled, quickly stammered, "Understood, sir. I promise—no more torture." Turning to his soldiers, he sounded the battle horn and ordered, "All troops, release the hostages. No more harm shall come to the people."

Theon chuckled. "That's the spirit. Unless, of course, you'd rather become an actual spirit, which I can arrange."

After returning to the land of the sun and moon worshipers, Theon changed out of his disguise into comfortable, armorless clothing. He then presented the God Set to the Southern King.

"Here is your Moonbow and Arrow of Flames as promised," Theon said humbly, handing the God Set to the Southern King. "Now, will you accept our proposal for an alliance?"

The King's eyes gleamed as he admired the Moonbow. He picked up the Arrow of Flames and examined it closely for authenticity, smiling in satisfaction—until he noticed the tip of the arrow.

"Something is missing," the King murmured. "The arrow must be stained with royal blood. Only then can it retain its powers."

"You... you wanted me to kill the neighbouring king?" Theon asked, his jaw dropping in shock.

"No..." Hercule interjected, "...he just wanted royal blood." The Southern King drove the arrow into Theon's back with a swift, gleaming thrust.

Theon gasped, his eyes widening as the pain coursed through him. He looked back at his one and only son. "Help!" he begged, Theon expecting immediate aid.

"Help, Pathetic fool; I always wanted some joy, some fame but was eternally overshadowed. You overshadowed me. But now I am overshadowed no longer. I am the rightful King of Niap Dnal, Hercule continued coldly, looking down at his father with a sense of accomplishment.

The Southern King stretched out his arm, and Hercule shook it resonantly. "I think this is where our arrangement ends. I kill your father, and I am assured permanent freedom from me and Quin-Chi."

VII
The Clash of Kings

When I woke up next, I found myself locked in a prison. The food was stale, smelling worse than a blocked toilet. A soft lapping sound interrupted the silence. Peering through the cell window, I saw Shadow—my dear panther. I slid my hand through the iron bars to rub his soft paws. The bars were cold and unyielding. Nearby, I heard the footsteps of a guard approaching. Quickly, I ushered Shadow away, careful not to alert the guard—this sequence of events repeated every night during my imprisonment. A part of me wondered if Renid was sending him to keep me sane. These moments became the best part of each day as I waited eagerly for Shadow's return.

I expected to remain in prison forever. Eventually, I lost track of the days, but I knew it had been over a month—a month of solitude. My only comfort came from knowing Renid hadn't revealed our connection to the Emperor of Gradam; otherwise, I would have been executed by now.

One day, I checked the window, but Shadow wasn't there. This continued for several days. Nothing brought me solace anymore. The only thing keeping me from despair was sheer willpower. I remembered my father's words: *"Where there's a will, there's a way."*

I suspected Renid had escaped and was worried about me. I guessed today was the day of the great battle: The Protectors versus the Black Jade Army. Faintly, I heard the eerie sounds of swords clashing, spears striking, and shields crashing. My suspicions were confirmed when my cell door creaked open. The guard unchained me.

"Today, boy, you're fighting against the Protectors. If luck's on your side, you might survive for a while. Take this sword and shield and that rusted armour over there. Want a spear or bow? Scavenge one from the dead soldiers. Get ready. The battle starts in ten minutes."

I quickly strapped on the armour and grabbed the sword and shield, though I had no intention of using them. Soon, a fat man led me onto the battlefield. The Protector's army arrived minutes later. I scanned their ranks, hoping to spot Renid, Hercule, Theon, TRR, or the Western King of Wadan. But I recognised no one. I was utterly alone. My mind raced to devise a plan, but the blaring of battle horns shattered my concentration.

The commander of the Protectors, Captain Zahir, roared, "Attack!" The soldiers moved forward, and I joined them to avoid being trampled. Then, I got an idea - as soon as I was near the front lines, I intensely collapsed, feigning death. Moments later, two bodies fell on top of me, their warm blood trickling down my neck—evidently, they were indeed dead. To anyone else, I was just another lifeless corpse.

Occasionally, soldiers stepped on me, each impact sending waves of pain through my body. I bit my tongue to stifle any cries, knowing a single sound could cost me my life. Hours passed, filled with the horrors of war—blood, death, pain, and the endless screams of the dying.

At last, I heard the words I'd been waiting for from both sides: "Retreat! This is pointless!" Twenty minutes later, the battlefield was silent. I lay alone amid a sea of corpses and a river of blood.

Rising from the blood-soaked ground, I ran toward the gates of Niap Dnal. After cleansing myself in a nearby river, I entered Theon's palace. Wandering into the meeting room, I saw a portrait on the wall. Below it was an inscription:

Emperor Theon of Niap Dnal

15 August 1432 – 31 May 1479

I was stunned. It took me a moment to process the truth: I had lost so many—Dad, Uncle, and now Theon. Grief weighed heavily on me as I made my way to the room assigned to me. Inside, I found Renid crying. Quietly, I shut the door behind me.

"Renid," I called softly.

He stopped crying, muttering, "Oh, how I wish you were real. But after losing everything, how could I expect anything better?"

"Renid, I *am* real," I said, concerned for his mental state.

He turned to me. "If you're real, then touch me. If I can feel you, then you're real."

I rushed to his side, embracing him. "It's okay. I'm here, I'm real, and most of all, I'm alive."

"How? A soldier showed me your body—your neck was bleeding," Renid whimpered, disbelief clouding his voice.

"I pretended to be dead. A fallen soldier landed on me, covering me with his blood. It made me look lifeless so they wouldn't target me," I explained.

Renid sniffed. "Hercule and Theon managed to steal the legendary God Set from the Southern King. But Theon died in the process."

"I know, brother. We've lost another brave warrior—a great man. But worry not. He's in a better place now, and he'll tell Father what a remarkable person you've become. Father didn't truly die, did he? He still lives within us. Theon will be avenged, along with our father. Quin-Chi will pay the price for what he's done."

I spoke with newfound resolve, determination burning in my heart.

"Swish, you really are the eternal optimist. The best thing to happen is obtaining the Moonbow and the Arrow of Fire—the legendary duo."

"The Moonbow and the Arrow of Fire? Those are real?" I asked, astonished. "I thought they were just myths."

"No, they're as real as it gets," Renid replied solemnly.

"So, what's the plan for the great battle?" I asked.

"That's a secret. Phase three of the earlier plan. You'll see it live on the battleground."

The next day, I prepared for the battle. Fully armed, we gathered on the field where the Protectors and the Black Jade Army gathered their forces. It was destined to be a monumental clash. Quin-Chi's voice boomed across the battlefield, amplified by a Voice Amplifying Machine (VAM).

"Ah, the mighty Swish and Renid. I've longed for this day. This battle will decide the fate of the world. Once the Protectors fall, global domination will be mine. Even if the other kingdoms unite, they'll crumble under the might of the Black Jade Army!"

Quin-Chi continued, his voice dripping with disdain. "You cannot win. We outnumber you nearly ten to one."

Renid replied sharply through his own VAM. "We may be outnumbered, but battles are won with skill and strategy, not brute force and sheer numbers."

He gave a sharp whistle. A thunderous crash and feral roars followed. I turned to see crates exploding open, releasing an array of beasts—lions, tigers, panthers, and eagles.

In an instant, Shadow, my loyal panther, leapt to my side, clad in armour from whiskers to tail. I mounted him, commanding, "Run, Shadow! Attack!"

At my signal, our troops mounted the animals and charged into the heart of the enemy army, catching them off guard. Suddenly, rocks began to rain down from above. I looked up, realising our eagles—Pecker, Fetcher, and Chainsaw—were dropping them. The heavy stones struck with force, knocking soldiers unconscious.

Our animal allies pushed deep into the enemy ranks, spreading chaos. Soldiers panicked and fled, causing a stampede. Forced into tighter clusters for protection, they became easy targets.

Renid's voice echoed through the VAM. "Retreat!"

Confused by the order, I hesitated but obeyed, pulling back to a safe distance. A few seconds later, a blazing arrow streaked through the sky, its flames trailing like a comet. It struck the cluster of soldiers, triggering a series of loud explosions.

As I watched the destruction, Renid explained, "The eagles were dropping explosives. These only detonate when ignited. Once the soldiers were packed together, TRR used the Moonbow and the Arrow of Fire. His aim is legendary—he didn't miss. The clustered explosives ignited all at once, maximising the damage. The Panthers were just a distraction."

Across the field, Quin-Chi's frantic voice shouted through his VAM, "Attack! Black Jade Army, don't fail me!"

What followed was a gruelling, three-day battle. Both armies were pushed to their limits. Exhaustion and injuries forced us into brutal hand-to-hand combat. By then, many of our panthers were either dead or wounded, and the eagles could no longer navigate the smoke-filled skies.

The legendary Arrow of Fire was lost in the explosion, destroying part of the God Set in the process. Its legacy, once indomitable, had been undone by its own power.

As the fighting wore on, the battlefield was littered with bodies. The loss of life was astounding. Taking Renid's VAM, I called out, "Stop!"

My voice echoed across the field, and swords clashing gradually ceased. "This fight is pointless! All we are doing is reducing the numbers. The true fight is between Quin-Chi, Renid, and me—not everyone else. This isn't a battle; it's a massacre. Quin-Chi lay down your weapons and tend to your wounded. We'll face you directly. Whatever the outcome, no one else will interfere."

Renid and I mounted Shadow and rode to Quin-Chi's unguarded castle. At the entrance, I dismounted, placing a hand on Shadow. "As much as I'd like you by our side, this is something we must do alone."

We entered the throne room to find Quin-Chi seated, waiting. His gaze settled on Renid.

"So, which of you is older—Renid or Swish?" he asked grimly.

Renid's expression hardened. "That doesn't matter. We're both here to kill you."

"Answer the question, arrogant boy," Quin-Chi sneered.

I stepped forward, my voice laced with anger. "You've got some nerve calling my younger brother arrogant in front of me." I drew my sword, ready for whatever comes next.

Quin-Chi's eyes flashed with malice. "So, Swish, you're the elder. That makes you the first heir to the throne. I challenge you to a duel to the death. If you win, my entire empire is yours."

"And if I lose?" I asked, my voice trembling.

Quin-Chi smiled coldly. "Then you die—it's a battle to the death. Renid dies as well. I'll conquer the Protectors, who will be leaderless, and then dominate the world. So yes, the fate of the world hinges on our duel. Three, two, one—begin."

I swallowed hard as Quin-Chi lunged at me with his sword. He had the advantage in height, strength, training, and experience. Still, I held my ground, fighting back with everything I had. Quin-Chi momentarily lost his balance, and I seized the chance, striking at him six times and throwing a powerful punch. Only the punch landed, but he showed no signs of fatigue. I, however, was exhausted, collapsing backwards and sinking to my knees.

Quin-Chi continued delivering blow after blow, each more powerful than the last. I knew I was being finished. This was the end. With a heavy heart, I muttered, "I'm sorry, Renid. Because of me, you'll die too."

Just then, a dagger plunged into Quin-Chi's back, piercing his heart. It was Renid. Behind him, I saw TRR, who had saved me and Renid.

"M..." Quin-Chi, his strength fading, looked up at me and whispered, "My boss... will k... kill you..."

My jaw dropped. "Quin-Chi... has a boss?"

Renid shook his head and sighed, "Desperate people say desperate things. He's probably trying to haunt you with his last words. A lousy trick." He turned to TRR and added, "I can't thank you enough. Come here, hug me," pulling him into a grateful embrace.

Suddenly, we heard a sharp thrust. A hooded figure had appeared, driving a sword through TRR. "Prince Renid," he sneered, "are you certain Quin-Chi didn't have a boss?"

TRR collapsed to the floor. My eyes widened as I screamed in horror.

"Who are you?" I demanded, choking back tears.

"Just your worst nightmare," the hooded figure replied calmly.

"Why did you kill my friend... my family? What did I ever do to you? Why are you against us?" I cried, desperate for answers.

"Nothing, really—other than jealousy." He removed his hood, revealing his dark, brooding, and evil face.

I dreaded this the most. It was a betrayal. It was Hercule.

"You traitor!" Renid lunged at Hercule, but it was not beneficial. Hercule lashed back furiously. I rushed forward as Hercule had Renid at his neck.

"What do you want?" I croaked in pain. "Anything—fame, wealth, land. Take the Protectors, but leave him."

"What I want is... suffering. Pain: pure and unruly pain. Pain with no remorse. Remember, you are at my mercy," he bellowed.

"You're crazy," Renid spoke, horrified, as he struggled to escape Hercule's grasp.

"Am I crazy? Am I a genius? A maniac? No difference. Try me. I am stronger than both of you combined. Do not try to defeat me. Your struggles are in vain. You and your bloodline are pathetic. All I want is to end your family permanently."

Behind Hercule, I saw a stabbed TRR desperately trying to stand up. My heart was filled with hope. Maybe TRR did not die in vain. Maybe.

My thoughts were interrupted by the entry of a series of men in different robes. One of them stabbed TRR once and for all. Blood leaked all over the floor as Hercule said, "I can kill you now and then dominate the world, but where's the fun in that? Let's play a little game instead."

Before I could react, his soldier knocked me unconscious. I was helpless. My eyes were flashing with painful memories—death upon death.

When I woke, I noticed my legs were bound to an antique chair. I could feel its rims as I looked around the well-lit palace room, where I saw multiple portraits with golden inscriptions. In front of me sat Hercule. He said, "You have one chance. Lose it, and all your friends die. Win, and I voluntarily leave you with the entire empire." His men surrounded me. I could not help but notice his weakness. I was bound, yet he wanted men in the vicinity. He was still scared of losing. I needed to exploit that.

I saw freshly mown grass through the nearby window and a unique tiling pattern of interlocking squares. Thirty-two men were standing on them in robes of white and black. Some men were on dashing horses, while others wore different clothes and stood on chairs with swords. Then it hit me. I was playing Chess. Or, to be precise, Human Chess.

In the window to my left, I saw a massive cage containing a group of people: Renid, the Western King of Wadan, the Southwestern King of Aliened and my beloved Shadow. In front of me was an antique grid with alternating tiles of white marble and obsidian. The squares had golden borders and were encrusted with diamonds on the edges. On them stood pieces of dried oak wood. Each piece would have taken months to carve. They were encrusted with rubies for white and sapphires for black. Beside them, two glass hourglasses stood, each the size of an adult palm. The falling sand was replaced with mashed-up tea and coffee leaves, emitting a more potent fragrance the less time was left.

I finally looked at Hercule. I met his gaze, loathing him from the depths of my heart. I despised him in every way, yet I was facing him. *A battle of doom,* my mind raced. Only one person will emerge when the sun dawns: me or Hercule. It would either be the evil monarch who would rule the world or a young boy liberated from a cruel tyranny. The choice was mine. I knew I had no chance, but all this pain stirred something within me.

Despair clawed at my throat. Thirst burned my lips. I needed to play. It mattered to millions of people. It mattered for Renid. It mattered for the friends I had made along the way. I knew I had to do this. I glanced at my side one last time. Renid was asleep, yet his expression remained resolute.

I looked at his face one last time. His uncanny features resembled my father's. It reminded me why I had started this challenging journey: to kill Quin-Chi. He killed my father. I killed him. Was the job done? I asked myself. My dad never made himself the priority—it was always the people. The countless lives that couldn't save themselves. Now it was my turn, I thought. It was time to seize the opportunity and win.

Hercule mockingly spoke, "We will play three games. The winner is the one who wins two of the three games. If and when you lose, I will kill everybody you know and love." His voice dripped with arrogance. He was confident. Maybe he was overconfident. I could use that to my advantage.

With newfound determination and resolve, I picked up the Queen's Pawn and placed it in front of me. Hercule responded by mirroring my move. Time slipped by as I thoughtfully played moves, and Hercule responded within seconds. Every time a piece was captured, a man on the human board was violently murdered. At this point, we had reached a crucial juncture.

I had two options: play it safe and Retreat, or sacrifice my knight and go for an attack. Logic dictated that there was no point in taking risks because millions of lives were at stake. I played it safe and retreated my knight. My hands were sweaty. For each move, I thought two sequences ahead, calculating every possibility.

But it was futile. Ultimately, he forced my King into a corner, just as he had betrayed and forced us into a corner. The game was lost. My King would have been mated in two moves. Just then, Hercule tipped over his own King with a mocking laugh.

"I have won the game, but the point is yours. I resign."

I was stunned. Although Hercule had won the game, he resigned and gave me the point, as he was sure that he would win next two games.

My hopes soared. I only needed one last win to save everyone and fulfil my dad's dying wish. I had to win. But it wouldn't be as easy as I had imagined. Hercule was ten times the player I was. Yet he had one major flaw—his undeniable arrogance.

❧

The second game began, and I had the black pieces this time. I played cautiously, avoiding all attacks and hardly making any of my own. This time, I played so well that I even managed to find a massive defect in his defence. Unfortunately, my pieces were in defensive positions so that I could do nothing.

Minutes later, Hercule blundered his bishop, and I took it. Several moves later, he made a slight inaccuracy. Exploiting it might have let me win, but it was risky and would open up my King to attacks. I remembered my original strategy: play defensively.

Slowly but surely, I began turning the tide in my favour. I noticed it. In a couple of moves, I could beat Hercule. The gold on the board shimmered as the scent of coffee grew stronger. My palms grew sweatier by the second. He had six pieces on the board, and I had thirteen. A part of me was still frightened. Hercule's face remained smug, his expression as arrogant as ever.

Towards the end, he forced all my pieces into the corners of the board and sacrificed his queen. Four moves later, he won.

He grinned and cackled, his laughter echoing through the room.

I looked below and saw multiple dead bodies piled up in a corner. His arrogance shocked me. He was ready to sacrifice his men just to gloat.

I hoped I could survive. For my sake. For Renid's sake. And for my dad.

☙

One last match. It all came down to this **final match.** My stomach churned. This was Hercule's final gambit. He knew he would win from the start. This was all to show me who the boss was.

I remembered the last thing my father wrote to me in his final letter: *"I will die protecting our people and our land. But remember, even in death, I am always with you."*

This was no longer for Renid or me. I have to also think about what's best for the people. Hercule had killed far too many people for his good. He had won time and time again. Now, it was my turn. It was about time I showed him I was no fool. I would die to save my people.

I was playing with the white pieces once more. This time, there was no room for defence. I needed aggression. The jewel-encrusted pieces reflected the light as I moved. I played with total aggression this time, sacrificing my horse and two more pawns.

At this stage, I recognised the position. It was the same one we had reached a couple of hours ago. This was the crucial juncture of our first game. Last time, I had retreated, and Hercule proceeded to checkmate my King in ten moves (although he resigned). I was sure he wouldn't resign this time.

So I decided to go for the invasion. I sacrificed my other horse also to open up his King. But this was a significant mistake on my part—Hercule could win in three moves.

I wasn't sure if he had realised it, but I decided to gamble everything for a chance. Through his severe arrogance, he hadn't noticed the mistake I made. I went ahead and risked my queen.

He had to take the gambit. If he didn't, I would lose. Hercule stalled. He thought and thought for over ten minutes, although it felt like an eternity.

In the end, he grinned. Hercule's eyes glimmered with satisfaction.

He said, "I could win now; or take your queen and slowly dominate the game as I go." He overlooked the plan in his ego. He took my queen. Now, he was sure to lose. Two moves later, I grinned as I silently spoke Check and Mate. His face looked aghast.

He looked at me menacingly; he was ready to kill me. He raised his dagger from his belt. I softly spoke, "Will you go back on your word? I thought you had a sense of pride. Remember, you gave me your word. A promise is a promise."

His eyes overflowed with sadness. The face that had shown arrogance moments earlier was now filled with despair. He dropped the blade. His final words were, "Kill me fast. End it now."

I did not disappoint. I picked up the blade and stabbed him in the heart. A fierce scream echoed as Hercule's body fell to the ground. He lay there, limp. I had done it.

I looked to my right and boldly commanded, "Guards, free them."

The cells were opened, and Renid ran to me. My vision blurred. I was exhausted. I looked up at the sky. The sun cast an orange glow, radiating between the mountains. I thought of my father.

I had fulfilled his final wish. Against all odds. My entire body ached. Through all the pain, the effort, and the sacrifice, I learned the actual value of life.

After losing my grandad, my dad, my uncle, Theon, and TRR, I doubted I had much left to lose. Thousands of our men died in the war, but millions of people were liberated from evil.

Hercule may have won the battle, but we won the war. The men and women who gave their lives would not die in vain. We would remember them deep in our hearts.

Whatever had happened today would soon become a sensation among the people. Nearby, hordes of people came to thank me.

Now that I owned most of the world's land, my life would become a constant target to assassins. The danger would always loom overhead, 'but we would have to overcome that' I reassured myself. But deep down, I knew this wasn't the end.

The world became reaccustomed to their new lives with Swish and Renid as the new kings of Gradam and nearby places. Meanwhile, somewhere in the shadows, another threat loomed.

A fierce and hoarse voice spoke:

"So, the Gradam Brothers think they can take my destined kingdom. I will show them."

The voice continued in a brooding fashion:

"Get ready my warriors, we have things to do and brothers to kill."

Author's Note To Reader

Thank you, dear and patient readers, for making it to the end. What you have read is invaluable to my heart, and I am deeply grateful for your time and support.

You haven't just read this book—you've experienced the highs and lows, the triumphs and sorrows, alongside the Gradam brothers. You've endured every loss and celebrated every victory with them.

But this is not the end of their journey. More significant challenges lie ahead, and the Gradam brothers, along with Shadow and the eagles, will rely on your support as they face what's to come.

Remember, this is only the beginning. There is so much more to discover in the lives of the Gradam brothers. Stay with me as their story continues to unfold.

I'd love to hear your thoughts about this book—your feedback means the world to me. Please share your experiences or comments at *my email id* _yuktkhetan@gmail.com_

Meet Yukt Khetan, a 12-year-old storyteller whose vivid imagination and love for books have inspired his debut as an author. Beyond reading, he is passionate about math and enjoys exploring the beauty of numbers. Yukt also has a keen interest in playing chess.

Yukt began writing with a charming goal: to buy his parents an ice cream with the royalty he earns. He loves reading and writing because they let him create entire universes—ones where homework doesn't exist!

Yukt shares, "Writing is like telling a story to a patient piece of paper. It never interrupts, but it also never claps. Tough crowd!"

Through his debut book, Yukt proves that big dreams can fit in small hands. Hopefully, this is just the beginning of his incredible adventure—one that will unfold through many more captivating stories and, of course, even more ice cream!